I Hate English!

by ELLEN LEVINE

Illustrated by STEVE BJÖRKMAN

SCHOLASTIC INC.
New York Toronto London Auckland Sydney

*For Virginia Kee and the real Mei Mei,
and all the good people at the
Chinatown Planning Council*
—E.L.

*For David, Kristi, and Michael,
who love books*
—S.B.

ISBN 0-590-42304-5

Text copyright © 1989 by Ellen Levine.
Illustrations copyright © 1989 by Steven Björkman.
All rights reserved. Published by Scholastic Inc.
BLUE RIBBON is a registered trademark of Scholastic Inc.

30 29 28   11 12 13 14 15 / 0

Printed in the U.S.A.   40

I hate English! Mei Mei said
in her head
in Chinese.

Mei Mei was smart in school.
In *her* school in Hong Kong.
                    In Chinese.

But her family moved to New York.
She didn't know why.
She didn't want to move.
And she said all that
                    in Chinese.

Chinatown in New York was OK.
People looked like people she knew.
People talked like people she knew.
        In Chinese.

In New York
in school
everything happened
        in English.

Such a lonely language.
Each letter stands alone
and makes its own noise.
        Not like Chinese.

Sometimes English letters fight each other.
"We will go on a class TRIP,"
the teacher said

                in English.

T-R-I-P, thought Mei Mei.
The letters "T" and "R" bang against
each other, and each keeps its own sound.
                Not like Chinese.

親愛

歡迎

Mei Mei loved Chinese.
Especially writing.
Fast strokes,
short strokes,
long strokes —
the brush, the pen, the pencil — all
seemed to fly in her hand. But that was
Chinese.

Mei Mei wouldn't speak in school.
Most of the time she understood
what her teacher said. But
everything was in English, and
Mei Mei wouldn't speak
English.

One day her cousin Bing took her to
the Chinatown Learning Center.
Students brought their homework for
help. But not Mei Mei. She wouldn't
work

in English.

Tutors helped the older ones with
their English. Mei Mei helped the
little ones with arithmetic.
She was good at arithmetic. Numbers
weren't English or Chinese.
They were just

numbers.

Mei Mei loved the Center. She talked
and listened and explained and
argued. She did everything

in Chinese.

She helped the Director set up the tables. She played Ping-Pong and checkers. She sang songs. She wrote letters to friends in Hong Kong.

All in Chinese.

Dear Yee Fong, she wrote in Chinese. *How would you like me to visit you?* She laughed as she finished the letter. Then she had to write the address

in English.

Silly post office in New York! she thought. Why can't they read

Chinese?

Mei Mei had a dream. She thought
about it at least once a day.
Sometimes twice or three times.
She told Bing about it.

In Chinese.

All the gang — Bing and Mona and
Shek and Leo and Ann — would go
on a plane to Hong Kong. On the
plane everybody would speak

Chinese.

Instead they went to Jones Beach.
With the Director, Mei Mei and her
friends rode on three trains and one bus.
They brought lunch, bathing suits, towels,
and empty pails. The trip took two
hours, and they talked and joked the whole
way

in Chinese.

Leo and Bing buried themselves in the sand.
Ann and Mona built a castle on top of them.
"Shek," said Mei Mei, "let's dig for
shellfish."
And off they went with their pails.
"You can't eat those," said the
lifeguard. Mei Mei smiled and
kept on digging. "He probably doesn't
know how to cook them," Shek said
in Chinese.

She was right. The Director made
a fire in the picnic area
and cooked the shellfish.
Nobody said a word.
Everybody was busy — very busy —
eating. At last Mei Mei looked up
and said, "Delicious!"
in Chinese.

And then one day a terrible thing
happened. A teacher came to the
Learning Center to help Mei Mei
with

English.

Who was this person with short hair
and blue eyes? And why was she
smiling? Mei Mei was afraid.
She wouldn't speak a word
in English or Chinese.

"Hello. I'm Nancy," the person said. She
pointed to an empty table.
"Let's sit down." Mei Mei understood the
teacher's

English.

The teacher had a book, and she read
a story. Mei Mei forgot that she
didn't want to listen. The story was
interesting, even if it was in

English.

It was about a boy who lived in
New York more than a hundred years ago.
His family wanted to move to
California.
Mei Mei knew about California. She
smiled to herself as she thought
about California

in Chinese.

The teacher read on. "The family
crossed the country in a covered wagon."
Covered wagon? thought Mei Mei.
She didn't know the words for
covered wagon

in Chinese.

Mei Mei didn't want to hear any more.
She didn't want English to have words
that she didn't know

in Chinese.

She felt sad, and a tear slid down her cheek. She didn't want the teacher to see. But the teacher did see and said, "Let's stop for today,"

in English.

That night in bed Mei Mei felt afraid
again. She wasn't sure why.
She felt she might lose something.
She felt she had lost something.
She felt she would lose something.
"Goodnight," her mother said
in Chinese.

"Goodnight," answered Mei Mei
without thinking,
in English.

And then she fell into a deep sleep.
She dreamt about Hong Kong.
In the dream she went to see Yee Fong.
But Yee Fong said, "Who are you?"

in English.

Who am I? dreamt Mei Mei. I don't
even remember my name. She woke up
shouting, "I am Mei Mei!"

in Chinese.

The next day Mei Mei was mad.
She stared at the teacher.
She glared at the teacher.
And then she said, "I don't care!"
to the teacher,

in English.

"Very good!" said Nancy. "I knew you
could speak

English."

"But I don't think you really want
to learn," Nancy continued. "And
that's too bad."

Why is it too bad? thought Mei Mei
in Chinese.

The teacher seemed to read her mind.
"Because in America
almost everything happens
                    in English.

"Don't you want to go to an American
movie? Don't you want to ask for
pizza? Don't you want to have an ice-cream
cone? Don't you want to read
the signs at the zoo? Don't you want
to talk with me? I want
to talk with you," said Nancy
                    in English.

Mei Mei turned away. She wanted to
tell Nancy that she liked her.
But all she could say was,
"I'm sorry."

In English.

Nancy suddenly jumped up.
"Get your coat," she said to Mei Mei.
"We are going to take a walk."
Mei Mei said good-bye to Shek
in Chinese.

On the street a strange thing happened.
Nancy didn't *ask* Mei Mei to talk.
Nancy didn't *care* if Mei Mei talked.
Nancy didn't *want* Mei Mei to talk!
Nancy was talking.

In English.

She told Mei Mei about her third-grade
teacher. She told Mei Mei about
her favorite book. She told Mei Mei
that she loved tomatoes and potatoes.
She told Mei Mei about
Mr. Schwarz, her dog. She told
Mei Mei *everything*, it seemed,

in English.

Mei Mei thought about *her* school.
She thought about *her* favorite book.
She thought about char siu bao, *her* favorite
food. And she thought about
Siu Fa, *her* cat.

In Chinese.

But Nancy wouldn't stop talking.
She went on and on and on.
"Forever talking!" yelled Mei Mei.

In English.

Nancy didn't seem to hear. She kept
on talking. She started reading the
store signs. She read the names
forwards...and backwards.
Sang Ping became *Gnip Gnas!*
Mei Mei became *Iem Iem!*
And still Nancy talked

in English.

"Stop!" cried Mei Mei. She couldn't stand it anymore. She felt invisible. *I want to talk!* she shouted, in English.

And before she could think about what
she was doing, Mei Mei began.
She talked about Children's Day
in Hong Kong.
"You get lots of presents."
She talked about the dragon dances
on Chinese New Year. She talked about her
street in Hong Kong and all her
friends nearby. She talked for
twenty-two minutes without stopping.

In English.

Nancy was laughing. And as Mei Mei
talked, Nancy laughed more and more.
Mei Mei started to smile.
Then
she laughed a little. And then she
shook with laughter. They both
laughed so hard
neither one could say a word
          in English or Chinese.

"Thank you," said Nancy as she gave
  Mei Mei a hug.
"For what?" asked Mei Mei,
  still laughing.
"For giving me," said Nancy,
"a present of

                                    English."

"You are welcome," said Mei Mei.
And to this day Mei Mei talks
                    in Chinese
                      and English
  whenever she wants.